Happy Birthday, Lonnie 2008
A wonderful story + most important
one to share with your grandchildren
In Christ,
Margaret

D1032650

THE PRINCE'S
POISON CUP

WRITTEN BY
R. C. SPROUL

ILLUSTRATED BY JUSTIN GERARD

Reformation Trust
PUBLISHING

A DIVISION OF LIGONIER MINISTRIES, ORLANDO, FLORIDA

THE PRINCE'S
POISON CUP

Text: © 2008 by R. C. Sproul
Illustrations: © 2008 by Justin Gerard

Published by Reformation Trust
      a division of Ligonier Ministries
      400 Technology Park, Lake Mary, FL 32746
      www.ligonier.org
      www.reformationtrust.com

ISBN-13: 978-1-56769-104-7

Printed in Mexico.

Creative direction and book design by Matt Mantooth.

Library of Congress Cataloging-in-Publication Data

Sproul, R. C. (Robert Charles), 1939-
  The prince's poison cup / by R.C. Sproul ; illustrations by Justin Gerard.
    p. cm.
  Summary: In order to persuade a child to take her bitter-tasting medicine when she is sick, her
grandfather tells her a story in which a prince saves the people from sin by drinking from a poi-
soned fountain.
  ISBN 978-1-56769-104-7
  [1. Christian life--Fiction. 2. Parables.] I. Gerard, Justin, ill. II. Title.
  PZ7.S7693Pt 2008
  [E]--dc22
                                2008026899

To Ella Ruth Cobb,

our delightful first great-granddaughter

- R. C. SPROUL

"Shall I not drink the cup

that the Father has given me?"

JOHN 18:11B

 NE MORNING not so long ago, in a snug house in a small town, a little girl was feeling sick. Her name was Ella Ruth, but her family simply called her Ella.

Ella had a bad tummy ache, so the doctor had given her some medicine. Ella's father poured some of the medicine into a spoon. But as soon as Ella saw the medicine, she frowned and said: "Oh, Daddy, this medicine looks yucky. Do I really have to take it?"

Her father smiled and said, "Yes, dear, you have to take your medicine if you want to get well."

So Ella worked up her courage and finished the medicine just as her father told her. But then she asked, "Daddy, why does medicine taste so bad if it's going to make us well?"

"Well," her father said, "that's a question that you should ask Grandpa. He always can answer your hard questions. He's coming to visit this afternoon. Get some rest so you'll be feeling better when he gets here."

Ella took a nap and woke up when Grandpa arrived. He hugged Ella and asked her how she was feeling, and Ella told him she was feeling better. Then she looked up at him and said, "Grandpa, may I ask you a question?"

Grandpa nodded and replied, "Of course, my dear."

"Grandpa, why is my medicine so yucky if it's going to make me well?"

Grandpa looked thoughtful. "That's a very good question, Ella," he said. "Some things that look or taste or smell wonderful are really awful. But sometimes things that seem terrible are actually very good. I even remember a story in which both of these strange things were true. Would you like to hear it?"

"Oh, yes!" Ella said. She loved the stories Grandpa told to explain things. So Grandpa sat down and Ella snuggled up close beside him. Grandpa began by saying:

ONCE UPON A TIME, there was a great King. He was called the King of Life because He had the power to make anything, even living things like plants, animals, and people. The King made a beautiful park filled with trees, streams, lakes, and meadows. Each day, the King came to the park and visited with His subjects, the people He had made. They were very happy as they walked together in the beauty of the park.

In the center of the park the King placed a fountain. Up from the fountain bubbled beautiful water that looked cool and sweet. But the King told His people: "You may drink from all the streams in the park, but you may not drink from the fountain. The water in the fountain will harm you. Do not drink it."

At first, the King's subjects enjoyed spending time with Him so much that they didn't even go close to the fountain. They loved the King and wanted to please Him. But they began to get curious. They wondered why He didn't want them to drink the water of the fountain, which looked so pure and refreshing.

One day a stranger in a long black cloak appeared in the park. The people didn't know it, but the stranger was the King's archenemy. He told the people that the water in the fountain wasn't bad at all. He said that if they would try it, the water would do wonderful things for them. It would make them as great as the King Himself.

By now the people were very curious about the water. It didn't seem fair that the King wouldn't let them drink from the fountain. So they decided to try it. The stranger filled a cup with the water from the fountain and gave it to the people, and they drank it.

But a terrible thing happened when the people drank the water—
their hearts turned to stone. After that, they no longer felt any love
for their King. They didn't even want to be with Him anymore.

They stopped coming to the park to spend time with Him. Instead, they moved to a desert far away from the park and built themselves a city. They called it the City of Man.

The King of Life was angry that the people had disobeyed Him. He knew that because of the people's terrible violation of His command, He would be justified in destroying their city. But the King still loved His people and felt sorry for them in their pain.

The King was very wise and had known that the people would drink from the fountain, and He already had a plan to help them. He went to His Son, who was the Prince of the kingdom, and said to Him, "I want You to help heal Our subjects."

At that point in the story, Ella stopped Grandpa and asked, "What did the King want the Prince to do?"

"It was an awful task," Grandpa said. "The King gave the Prince a golden cup and told Him to go to the City of Man. There, in the central plaza of the city, the Prince would find another fountain. But this fountain was not filled with sweet-looking water; it was filled with terrible poison. The poison was made up of the King's anger over the people's disobedience. One drop of the poison would kill a strong man. But the King told the Prince to use the golden cup to drink a whole cupful of the poison in the fountain. He said if the Prince would do that, His subjects would be healed and could come back to the park."

The Prince loved His Father and His people, and even though the mission sounded very hard, He was determined to fulfill it. So He started on a journey to the City of Man. Several of His friends went with Him.

On the way to the city, the Prince and His friends stopped by a pond. The Prince stared into the water, which was beautiful, calm, and blue. But as He continued to gaze into the water, something strange happened. In His mind, He saw a large cup filled with a dark, murky liquid. He knew that it was the cup of poison that His Father had commanded Him to drink.

The Prince closed His eyes and shook His head to get the picture of the awful cup out of His mind. For a moment, He thought about turning back. But He remembered the King's order. He had to go to the City of Man. He knew that was where the poison was.

When the Prince and His friends arrived in the city, they saw that it was a terrible place. The streets were dark and filled with mud and trash. Many of the homes were broken down, and the people were unfriendly and suspicious. Someone recognized the Prince as the Son of the King of Life. Because they no longer loved the King, the people began to treat the Prince quite badly. They shouted curses at Him, spat at Him, and taunted Him. Some even tossed rocks at Him or slapped Him as He passed.

The Prince trembled in fear and began to sweat. He loved His Father, but He couldn't help wondering if there was another way for the people to be healed. He wondered if He really had to drink the poison. He thought about the golden cup He was carrying and said to Himself, "I wish that I didn't have to drink from this cup."

As the Prince struggled with His fear, He remembered the words of His Father: "You must drink the cup. It's the only way to heal Our people." More than anything else, the Prince wanted to please the King. So right then and there He decided that He would not turn back but would drink the poison just as His Father had asked, no matter what pain and suffering it might cost Him.

The Prince's friends also became very frightened as the angry mob of people around them grew, and one by one they all ran away. Soon the Prince was all alone in the midst of the angry people, but He kept looking for the fountain that was full of poison.

Finally, the Prince entered a great plaza. In the center of the plaza was the fountain. And standing by the fountain was a man in a dark cloak. It was the King's archenemy, the one who had persuaded the people to drink from the fountain in the park.

The Prince approached the fountain. Without saying a word, He took out the golden cup His Father had given Him and held it out to the man. With a cruel smile, the man filled the Prince's cup with the water from the fountain and gave it to the Prince. The angry people of the city gathered around the fountain to see what would happen.

The Prince looked at the poison that filled His cup. It was dark, murky, and smelly. He was horrified and disgusted by it. He knew it would kill Him. But as He looked around at the faces of the angry people, He remembered that their stony hearts would be healed if He drank it.

He put His lips to the edge of the cup and began to drink. The poison tasted bitter. He wanted to spit it out. But He had promised His Father He would drink it all. The poison burned His throat, but He continued to swallow. He finished it all, right down to the last sip.

When the poison was all gone, the Prince bowed His head, closed His eyes . . . and died. He fell to the pavement beside the fountain. As He fell, the man in the dark cloak laughed with glee, for he thought he had killed the King's Son, and all the people gave a great shout of triumph.

Just then, someone else entered the plaza. This person wore a cloak that was a brilliant white, so bright no one could look at it. As He walked, the ground trembled. He approached the fountain, and as He came, the man in the dark cloak stopped laughing. In dismay, he tried to shield his eyes from the brightness of the newcomer's cloak, but it was impossible. He began to run away, and as he ran he screamed, "The King of Life has come! Run for your lives." All the people fled, hiding themselves in the alleys and doorways around the plaza.

The King stopped beside the body of the Prince. Kneeling down, He touched His Son. When He did, the Prince opened His eyes. He was alive again. The King of Life had brought the Prince back from death.

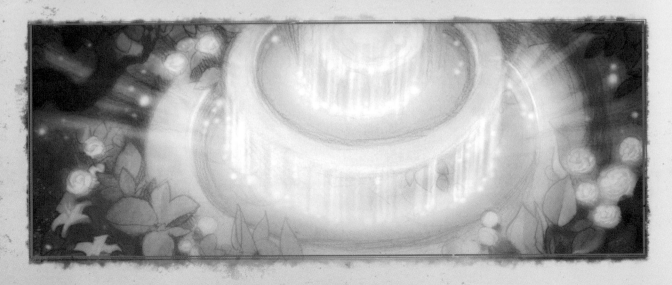

At that moment, the liquid bubbling up out of the fountain changed. No longer was it dark, murky poison. Now it was beautiful, clear, sweet water. The poison quickly drained away and the water filled the fountain. The water glittered in the sunlight and tinkled merrily as it fell into the fountain, and its sweet, fresh smell drifted across the plaza. The water seemed to be alive.

The Prince stood up and found the golden cup. Going to the fountain, He held it under the falling water and filled it to the brim. Then He turned to the people and held the cup out to them. "If anyone thirsts, let him come to Me and drink," He called out, and the blowing wind seemed to carry His words throughout the plaza and among the people watching from the shadows.

At that point, an amazing thing began to happen. The hearts of the people began to change, growing soft and warm once more. Some people's hearts remained hard and cold, but all around the plaza the hearts of men and women, boys and girls, old people and young children, rich merchants and poor workers were transformed.

Slowly, fearfully, those whose hearts were changed began to approach the fountain. They had always been repulsed by the horrible poison, but the Prince and the water He offered looked so glorious, they could not hold back.

Finally, one little boy approached the Prince and timidly took the cup. Then he took a small sip and swallowed the water. The people watched anxiously, but nothing terrible happened. Instead, the boy simply looked up at the King and the Prince with love and gratitude. He had been taught to hate Them, but now that hate was gone.

Seeing that nothing bad happened to the boy after he drank from the cup, many other people quickly followed his example. They no longer wanted to run and hide from the King. Instead, they came to drink from the golden cup, and all of those who drank praised the King and the Prince for healing them. They saw that the terrible poison the Prince had drunk was wonderful medicine for them. Although it tasted awful to the Prince and had caused Him to die, it had healed their stony hearts.

After that, the people joyfully began to visit the park once more, where they took great delight in walking with the King of Life and the Prince who had restored them to life again.

Grandpa leaned over to Ella and said to her: "Ella, I want you to remember that we get sick because of sin. That's why the medicine that makes our bodies well usually looks and tastes bad. But the Prince had to drink something far more terrible so that His people might be healed from the results of their disobedience. Each time you have to take bitter medicine, I want you to remember the story of the Prince's poison cup."

"I will, Grandpa," Ella promised. "And do you know what? I know another Prince who died for His people."

"Do you?" Grandpa asked, with a twinkle in his eye.

FOR PARENTS

We hope you and your child enjoyed reading *The Prince's Poison Cup*. The following questions and Bible passages may be helpful to you in guiding your child into a deeper understanding of the scriptural truths behind the book. Some of the questions and concepts may be too advanced for a younger child. If so, consider returning to the story as your child grows in his or her knowledge of the things of God.

WHO IS THE REAL KING OF LIFE?

> And God said, "Let the earth sprout vegetation, plants yielding seed, and fruit trees bearing fruit in which is their seed, each according to its kind, on the earth . . . Let the waters swarm with swarms of living creatures, and let birds fly above the earth across the expanse of the heavens. Let the earth bring forth living creatures according to their kinds—livestock and creeping things and beasts of the earth according to their kinds . . . Then God said, "Let us make man in our image, after our likeness. And let them have dominion over the fish of the sea and over the birds of the heavens and over the live stock and over all the earth and over every creeping thing that creeps on the earth." So God created man in his own image. (Genesis 1:11–27a)

> And this is the testimony, that God gave us eternal life, and this life is in his Son. (1 John 5:11)

IN THE STORY, THE KING OF LIFE WALKED WITH HIS PEOPLE IN A BEAUTIFUL PARK. WHERE DID GOD WALK WITH THE PEOPLE HE HAD MADE?

> And the LORD God planted a garden in Eden, in the east, and there he put the man whom he had formed. (Genesis 2:8)

> And they heard the sound of the LORD God walking in the garden. (Genesis 3:8a)

THE KING OF LIFE TOLD HIS PEOPLE NOT TO DRINK FROM THE FOUNTAIN IN THE PARK. WHAT DID GOD TELL HIS PEOPLE NOT TO DO?

> And the LORD God commanded the man, saying, "You may surely eat of every tree of the garden, but of the tree of the knowledge of good and evil you shall not eat, for in the day that you eat of it you shall surely die." (Genesis 2:16–17)

DOES GOD HAVE AN ARCHENEMY, SOMEONE LIKE THE MAN IN THE BLACK CLOAK?

> Now the serpent was more crafty than any other beast of the field that the LORD God had made. (Genesis 3:1)

And the great dragon was thrown down, that ancient serpent, who is called the devil and Satan, the deceiver of the whole world, he was thrown down to the earth, and his angels were thrown down with him. (Revelation 12:9)

THE MAN IN THE BLACK CLOAK LIED TO THE PEOPLE IN THE PARK. WHAT LIE DID SATAN TELL THE PEOPLE GOD HAD MADE?

But the serpent said to the woman, "You will not surely die. For God knows that when you eat of [the tree of the knowledge of good and evil] your eyes will be opened, and you will be like God, knowing good and evil." (Genesis 3:4–5)

IN THE STORY, WHEN THE PEOPLE DRANK WATER FROM THE FOUNTAIN, THEIR HEARTS TURNED TO STONE. WHAT HAPPENED TO THE PEOPLE WHO LISTENED TO SATAN'S LIE?

So when the woman saw that the tree was good for food, and that it was a delight to the eyes, and that the tree was to be desired to make one wise, she took of its fruit and ate, and she also gave some to her husband who was with her, and he ate. Then the eyes of both were opened, and they knew that they were naked. And they sewed fig leaves together and made themselves loincloths. And they heard the sound of the LORD God walking in the garden in the cool of the day, and the man and his wife hid themselves from the presence of the LORD God among the trees of the garden. (Genesis 3:6–8)

Sin came into the world through one man, and death through sin, and so death spread to all men because all sinned. (Romans 5:12)

IN WHAT WAYS IS THE REAL WORLD LIKE THE CITY OF MAN?

"The light has come into the world, and people loved the darkness rather than the light because their works were evil." (John 3:19)

"In the world you will have tribulation." (John 16:33b)

For the creation was subjected to futility . . . the creation itself will be set free from its bondage to corruption and obtain the freedom of the glory of the children of God. For we know that the whole creation has been groaning together in the pains of childbirth until now. (Romans 8:20–22)

IN THE STORY, THE KING OF LIFE HAD A SON WHO WAS THE PRINCE OF THE LAND. WHO IS GOD'S SON?

(CONT.)

These are written so that you may believe that Jesus is the Christ, the Son of God, and that by believing you may have life in his name. (John 20:31)

God is faithful, by whom you were called into the fellowship of his Son, Jesus Christ our Lord. (1 Corinthians 1:9)

THE PRINCE WAS TREATED VERY BADLY WHEN HE CAME TO THE CITY OF MAN. HOW DID PEOPLE TREAT JESUS WHEN HE CAME?

Then the soldiers of the governor took Jesus into the governor's headquarters, and they gathered the whole battalion before him. And they stripped him and put a scarlet robe on him, and twisting together a crown of thorns, they put it on his head and put a reed in his right hand. And kneeling before him, they mocked him, saying, "Hail, King of the Jews!" And they spit on him and took the reed and struck him on the head. (Matthew 27:27–30)

And those who passed by derided him, wagging their heads and saying, "Aha! You . . . save yourself, and come down from the cross!" So also the chief priests with the scribes mocked him to one another, saying, "He saved others; he cannot save himself.". . . Those who were crucified with him also reviled him. (Mark 15:29–32)

"Jesus, delivered up according to the definite plan and foreknowledge of God, you crucified and killed by the hands of lawless men." (Acts 2:23)

THE POISON THE PRINCE HAD TO DRINK WAS MADE UP OF "THE KING'S ANGER OVER THE PEOPLE'S DISOBEDIENCE." DOES GOD GET ANGRY ABOUT SIN?

For the wrath of God is revealed from heaven against all ungodliness and unrighteousness of men. (Romans 1:18a)

JESUS SAID THAT WHEN HE DIED ON THE CROSS, HE WOULD DRINK "THE CUP" HIS FATHER HAD GIVEN HIM (JOHN 18:11B). WHAT DOES IT MEAN FOR HIS PEOPLE THAT HE DRANK "A CUP" FULL OF GOD'S ANGER TOWARD THEM?

Whoever believes in the Son has eternal life; whoever does not obey the Son shall not see life, but the wrath of God remains on him. (John 3:36)

Jesus . . . delivers us from the wrath to come. (1 Thessalonians 1:10b)

WHEN THE PRINCE INVITED THE PEOPLE TO DRINK THE LIVING WATER FROM HIS CUP, THE WIND CARRIED HIS WORDS TO PEOPLE AROUND THE PLAZA. WHAT HELPS PEOPLE HEAR AND UNDERSTAND THE WORDS OF JESUS?

"When the Spirit of truth comes, he will guide you into all the truth." (John 16:13a)

And suddenly there came from heaven a sound like a mighty rushing wind, and it filled the entire house where they were sitting. . . . And they were all filled with the Holy Spirit. (Acts 2:2–4a)

DOES JESUS OFFER PEOPLE A "DRINK" OF SOME KIND?

Jesus answered her, "If you knew the gift of God and who it is that asks you for a drink, you would have asked him and he would have given you living water." (John 4:10)

On the last and greatest day of the Feast, Jesus stood and said in a loud voice, "If anyone is thirsty, let him come to me and drink." (John 7:37)

WHAT DOES IT MEAN TO DRINK FROM THE CUP JESUS OFFERS?

So Jesus said to them, "Truly, truly, I say to you, unless you eat the flesh of the Son of Man and drink his blood, you have no life in you. Whoever feeds on my flesh and drinks my blood has eternal life, and I will raise him up on the last day. For my flesh is true food, and my blood is true drink." (John 6:53–55)

"Whoever believes in me, as the Scripture has said, "Out of his heart will flow rivers of living water." (John 7:38)

"Believe in the Lord Jesus, and you will be saved." (Acts16:31a)

WHAT HAPPENS WHEN PEOPLE TRUST JESUS?

"And I will give you a new heart, and a new spirit I will put within you. And I will remove the heart of stone from your flesh and give you a heart of flesh." (Ezekiel 36:26)

"Whoever believes in him is not condemned, but whoever does not believe is condemned already, because he has not believed in the name of the only Son of God." (John 3:18)

"Truly, truly, I say to you, whoever hears my word and believes him who sent me has eternal life. He does not come into judgment, but has passed from death to life." (John 5:24)

ELLA SAID SHE KNEW ANOTHER PRINCE WHO DIED FOR HIS PEOPLE. WHO WAS SHE THINKING ABOUT?

For I delivered to you as of first importance what I also received: that Christ died for our sins in accordance with the Scriptures. (1 Corinthians 15:3)